USBORNE PARANORMAL GUIDES

GHOSTS?

Gillian Doherty

Designed by Stephen Wright
and Michèle Busby

Illustrated by Jeremy Gower,
Gary Bines and Nicholas Hewetson

Edited by Philippa Wingate

Consultants: John and Anne Spencer;
Caroline Watt, University of Edinburgh
Historical consultant: Anne Millard

Studio photography by Howard Allman
Digital images and textures created by John Russell

Series editor: Felicity Brooks

Picture research by Ruth King and Rebecca Gilpin

CONTENTS

INTRODUCTION

Some people believe that ghosts are merely figments of our imaginations. Others believe that they are visions, or apparitions, of the dead. Reports of ghostly activity can include non-visual experiences such as noises, smells or even sensations of coldness. There are also accounts of ghostly animals, ships and even ghosts of people who are still alive.

Ghost history

The earliest ghost reports are from over 2000 years ago. One early sighting was recorded by Pliny, a Roman writer. He told how in the 2nd century AD, a figure in chains appeared to Athenodorus, a Greek philosopher. The figure beckoned and he followed it outside, where it disappeared. The next day, when the area where it had disappeared was dug up, a skeleton bound in chains was revealed.

Case studies

Since most ghosts appear infrequently and their appearances are difficult to predict, attempts to prove that they exist have been largely unsuccessful. Ghost investigators have to rely on people's accounts for their evidence. Even if people are telling the truth, there could be other explanations for what they have experienced.

This book contains eight case studies of ghostly visitations. They range from classic historical hauntings to more modern ghostly sightings. Each is followed by an assessment which picks out the key facts of the story and explores possible explanations. It's up to you to decide what you believe.

This picture shows two 16th-century magicians, known as conjurors, calling up a spirit from the dead.

Case study one: A ROMAN INVASION

Date: 1953 and 1957
Place: The Treasurer's House, York, England
Witnesses: Harry Martindale and Joan Mawson

THE EVENTS

Harry put down his tools. He could hear an eerie noise, which seemed to be coming from deep within the walls. He was installing central heating in the cellar of a building called the Treasurer's House, so he assumed that it must be the sound of a radio in the building above.

An eerie noise

The sound grew steadily louder. Then, suddenly, a helmet bulged out of the wall. Harry stepped back in horror, tumbling from the ladder he was standing on. He scuttled into the corner of the cellar and watched in astonishment as a figure wearing a strange uniform and blowing a trumpet emerged. Behind him came a huge carthorse, followed by more figures who looked like soldiers.

The cellar where Harry was working

Figures wearing strange uniforms appeared from the wall of the cellar where Harry Martindale was working.

Missing legs

As the sound of the trumpet echoed around the cellar, Harry realized that it was the noise he had heard a few seconds before. He crouched down to observe the unexpected intruders.

Soldier after soldier trudged by. As they did, Harry noticed that, from the knees down, their legs disappeared into the floor. But when they crossed a section of the cellar where there was a hole in the floor, Harry caught a brief glimpse of their feet.

Military dress

The soldiers didn't pay any attention to Harry, so he had plenty of time to get a good look at them. They were armed with round shields, spears, short swords and daggers. Their feet dragged heavily along the ground and they seemed tired, as if returning from a battle or a long march.

The soldiers' bodies looked solid, though Harry guessed that they were far from being real.

The remains of a Roman sword and dagger, like the ones Harry saw the soldiers carrying

The last trumpet

Harry watched the trumpeter at the head of the procession cross the cellar and melt into the opposite wall. The sound of the trumpet lingered even though the trumpeter could no longer be seen. It was only as the last soldier disappeared that the sound finally ceased.

Other reports

Alone again, Harry wasted no time in rushing upstairs, where he met the curator who looked after a museum in the Treasurer's House. Seeing Harry's agitation, the curator guessed immediately what had happened. "By the look of you, you've seen the Romans, haven't you?" he said.

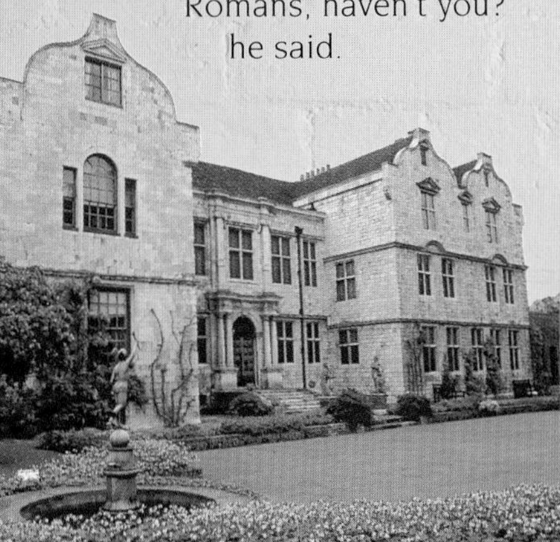

The Treasurer's House, York Minster

Harry was taken aback at this remark, but, at the curator's suggestion, he wrote down what he could remember about the incident. The curator then showed him two similar reports written by visitors who claimed to have seen the Romans. Harry was relieved to find that he was not alone in his experience.

Case study one: A ROMAN INVASION

A Roman road

In 1954, the year after Harry saw the Romans, archaeologist Peter Wenham began to excavate Roman remains beneath the Treasurer's House. He discovered what he believed to be a Roman road called the Via Decumana a little way below the modern floor of the cellar.

Part of the road had accidentally been exposed during earlier renovations to the house in around 1900. Significantly, this was the area where Harry had been able to see the soldiers' feet. It was as if the soldiers that Harry had seen had been walking along the old Roman road.

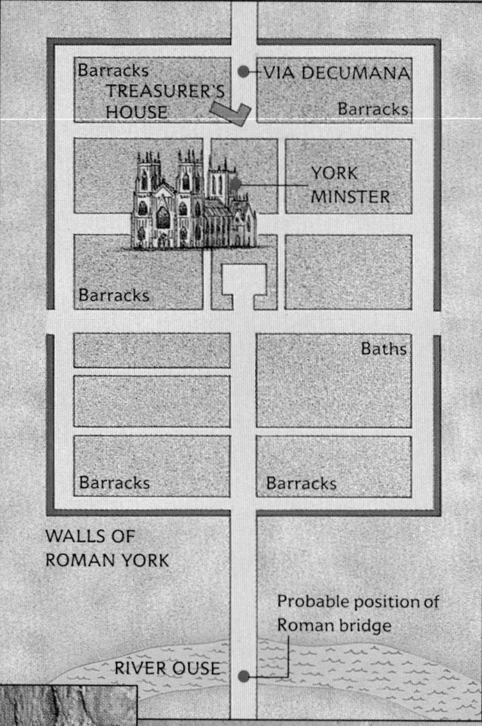

This map shows the position of the Roman roads around the Treasurer's House.

A Roman column base was exposed during renovations to the Treasurer's House in around 1900.

This diagram shows the hole in the cellar floor where Harry saw the Romans' feet.

The wrong shields

Initially, Harry's description of round shields cast doubt on his claims. The Roman foot soldiers, known as legionaries, in York would have been expected to use rectangular shields. However, in the 2nd century, when the surface of the Via Decumana exposed in the cellar dates from, the Roman army was made up of legionaries and soldiers called auxiliaries. The auxiliary soldiers used round shields.

A rectangular shield like the ones carried by Roman foot soldiers

A round shield like the ones used by auxiliary soldiers in Roman armies

Going public

For some reason, Harry's story was not made public until 1974, over 20 years after his experience. It was only then that Joan Mawson, a caretaker at the Treasurer's House during the 1950s, told people about her own contact with Romans in the cellar.

The sound of hooves

It was on a Sunday evening in 1957 that Joan first saw the Romans. She went to the cellar of the Treasurer's House to check on the boiler. At first, her dog, a white bull terrier, ambled ahead of her. Then, suddenly, the dog ran howling from the cellar.

As Joan entered a narrow tunnel that led into the cellar, she thought she heard the sound of horses' hooves. A moment later she became aware of someone, or something, behind her. She turned and froze in terror. A group of Roman soldiers on horseback towered above her. She flattened herself against the wall, terrified that they would trample her underfoot, but the soldiers didn't seem to notice her.

Case study one: A ROMAN INVASION

Weary troops

Joan saw the soldiers on two other occasions. Both times, she was alone in the cellar. The second time she saw them, they were splattered with mud and looked very tired.

On the third occasion, the soldiers looked extremely dishevelled and were slumped wearily over their horses' necks.

Many years passed before Joan told anyone about her experiences.

A mystery guest

There is at least one other story relating to Romans seen at the Treasurer's House. It dates from the 1920s and has been passed down by word of mouth.

During a party given by a man named Frank Green, who owned the house at that time, a female guest went to the cellar, perhaps during a game of hide-and-seek. She found her way barred by someone dressed as a soldier. Many of the guests at the party were dressed up in costumes, but there was something odd about the incident. She mentioned it to the host, but Frank was insistent that there was nobody at the party who was dressed in that way. Could it have been one of the Romans?

The soldier raised his hand to block the guest's way.

Case study one: THE ASSESSMENT

The details of Harry Martindale's story are very intricate and he appears to have the support of other witnesses. But did he really see ghosts, or are other explanations more likely?

Historical detail

If Harry was aware of the Roman history of the place or its ghostly stories, he may have allowed his imagination to run wild. Yet he couldn't have known about the round shields without a great deal of research.

Harry Martindale, many years after his ghostly experience

However, if he did make up the story, it could be coincidence that his account fit in with historical facts. York has strong Roman links, so any research may reveal a match between a ghostly experience and earlier historical events or remains.

This picture shows the cast from a film called Spartacus. Harry claims that his only ideas about what Romans looked like came from such films. However, the costumes in this film look very different from those he saw in the cellar.

Unreliable memories

Joan Mawson's account adds weight to Harry's, but the delay before each of them came forward makes their stories less believable. Over a period of time, people's memories can change and new details can be added. Also, the fact that Joan didn't tell anyone at the time of her experience makes it impossible to check her story.

Prompting

If the curator had discussed the other ghostly reports with Harry before asking Harry to write down his story, Harry may have mixed up his own experiences with those told by the curator. This kind of confusion could account for the similarities between such stories.

Universal (U.I.P.)

Case study two: ECHOES OF BATTLE

Date: 1642 – 1643
Place: Edgehill and Kineton, England
Witnesses: Multiple witnesses

THE EVENTS

The dull, regular thud of distant drums began to draw closer. It was accompanied by agonized groans of pain and terror. Steadily, the noise became louder until it grew to a deafening roar.

Battle cries

In the middle of the field, a group of shepherds stood trembling. Terrifying noises echoed all around them, though they could see nothing. Then, suddenly, they were stopped dead in their tracks by an incredible sight.

In the air above, a terrible battle was raging. Soldiers on horseback were thrusting and slashing with their swords. Cannons belched forth clouds of thick, black smoke and muskets fired out deadly shots.

Soldiers appeared in the sky above the shepherds.

Clashing armies

The shepherds crouched down in the grass. A few moments before, they had been quietly tending their sheep. Now, suddenly, they were witnesses to an extraordinary vision.

Through the smoke, they could see people carrying flags which they recognized. The first battle of the English Civil War, known as the Battle of Edgehill, had been fought on that spot in October 1642, only a few months before. Had the troops from this battle somehow returned to fight again?

A strange story

The shepherds' ordeal lasted several hours. Then the armies vanished as abruptly as they had appeared.

The men hurried to the town of Kineton and woke up Mr. Wood and Mr. Marshall, two respected members of the community. When Mr. Wood heard their tale, he thought that they must be drunk or crazy. But he also knew some of the men personally and, sensing their genuine fear, felt he ought to take them seriously.

A second sighting

The next night, the shepherds took a group of people to the place where they had seen the vision. After half an hour of waiting, the eerie battle began again. It was as violent and terrifying as before.

The crashing of swords and pikes rang out as the soldiers locked together in deadly battle.

Disappearing horsemen

After these sightings, the armies were not seen for several nights, but then a group of strangers to the town reported meeting soldiers of a similar description on the road. They said that a troop of horsemen had ridden past them and had then sunk mysteriously into the ground. When the newcomers told their tale, the townspeople mocked them. But they were quickly forced to change their attitudes.

An engraving of the ghostly battle from a 17th-century pamphlet that decribed the strange events

A town in terror

On January 4th, in the middle of the night, the people of Kineton woke up trembling as the battle began again. Some hid in corners, while others lay sweating under their covers. Only a few brave individuals peered out of their windows. They saw horsemen raging along the road.

Driven away

The next night, a small group gathered to stand guard at the town's gates. At midnight, the soldiers appeared again. For many people the experience was too much. The next day, they gathered up a few belongings and left Kineton.

Kineton is about 2 miles (3km) from the Edgehill site.

Informing the king

Mr. Marshall decided to take charge of the situation. He went to Oxford to inform King Charles. Intrigued by the story, the king sent some men to Edgehill to investigate.

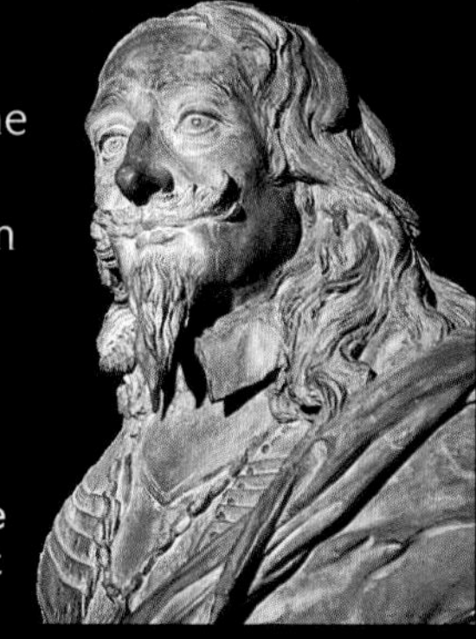

A bust of King Charles I, whose troops fought at Edgehill

Familiar faces

The king's men were amazed at the sight that met them the following Saturday. They recognized the uniforms of their own troops and even the faces of some of the soldiers. They realized with horror that several of the soldiers, including their friend Sir Edmund Verney, were men who had died at the Battle of Edgehill several months previously.

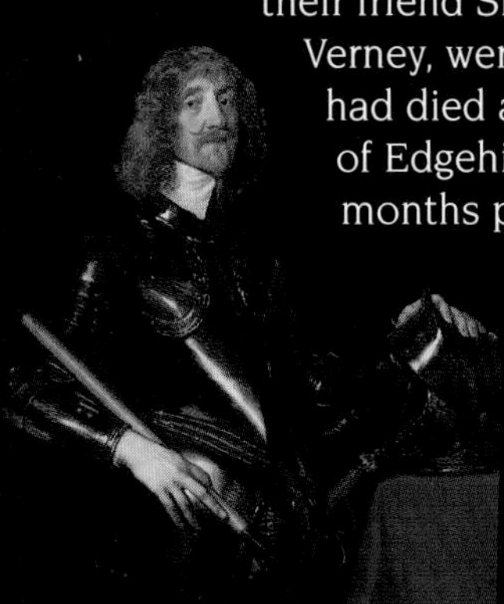

A portrait of Sir Edmund Verney, who died in the Battle of Edgehill

A peaceful end

The armed phantoms continued to appear, to the distress of the residents of Kineton. Finally, someone suggested that the apparitions might be the restless souls of the dead. A search of the battlefield revealed a number of unburied bodies. Shortly after, when the bodies had been buried, the visions finally ceased.

The site of the Battle of Edgehill today

The English Civil War

In the 1640s, England was divided by a struggle for power between King Charles I and Parliament. This led to the outbreak of civil war in 1642.

The first major conflict of the Civil War took place at Edgehill in October 1642. Neither side had a clear victory and many soldiers were killed. Those who witnessed the apparitions at Edgehill believed that they had seen a ghostly reenactment of this battle.

Oliver Cromwell, pictured at the front of this group of horsemen, was the leader of the Parliamentarians.

Reports of such vivid and lengthy apparitions, and ones with so many witnesses are rare. Yet it is difficult to confirm the facts of a case that happened so long ago.

Superstitious times

In the 17th century, belief in the supernatural was more widespread than it is today. Across Europe, many hundreds of people were drowned or burned as witches. Belief in fairies and magic was commonplace, and ghosts were often reported. Ghosts also appeared in the literature of the era, featuring in two of Shakespeare's most famous plays, *Macbeth* and *Hamlet*. Perhaps the Edgehill story was invented by people caught up in this superstitious atmosphere.

A scene from a modern performance of Shakespeare's play *Macbeth, which features three witches*

Political pamphlets

The ghostly battle was described in two pamphlets written in the 17th century. However, these pamphlets are not necessarily reliable accounts of what actually happened. Pamphlets sometimes had a political purpose. In fact, the author of these pamphlets is openly political, calling for an end to the Civil War, and for God to bring King Charles to his senses.

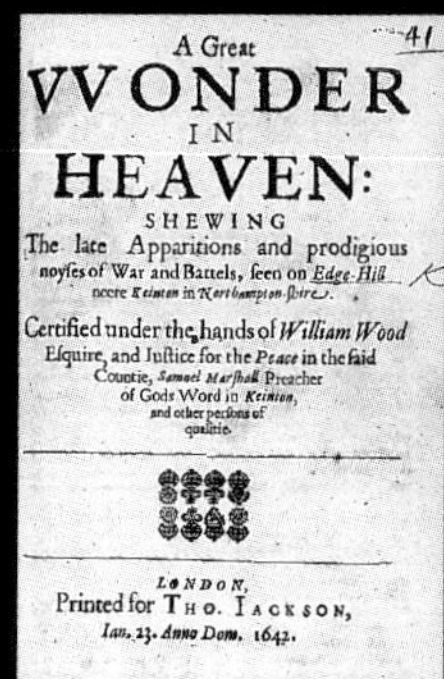

A Great
VVONDER
IN
HEAVEN:
SHEWING
The late Apparitions and prodigious noyses of War and Battels, seen on Edge-Hill neere Keinton in Northampton-shire.

Certified under the hands of *William Wood* Esquire, and Justice for the *Peace* in the said Countie, *Samuel Marshall* Preacher of Gods Word in *Keinton*, and other persons of qualitie.

LONDON,
Printed for THO. IACKSON,
Ian. 23. Anno Dom. 1642.

A 17th-century pamphlet which describes the ghostly battle

ACTION REPLAYS

Some paranormal investigators have suggested that certain apparitions may be recordings of events from a previous era. They believe that these are like video or sound recordings, but what is played back is a scene, sounds or sensations from the past.

Frozen in time

The term "recording ghosts" is given to apparitions that always appear in the same place. They seem unaware of the people who witness them and of their modern surroundings. It's as if the ghosts are fixed in time and space.

One explanation that has been offered for ghosts walking through walls is that this type of ghost moves around a building as it was in its own time. People have suggested that when a ghost walks through a wall, it is because there used to be a door there.

This scene from the film *The Frighteners* illustrates the popular view of a ghost's ability to pass through walls.

Universal (U.I.P.)

How are recordings made?

When we are afraid or stressed, we produce a high level of emotional energy. One theory offered to explain recording ghosts suggests that under certain conditions this energy is stored at a particular location. So, if someone is distressed, they may leave an emotional imprint, or recording, which lingers after their death.

No clear scientific argument has been offered to explain how this happens. It has been suggested that the presence of a particular mineral in the walls or surroundings may be relevant. For example, the mineral quartz produces an electric field when pressure is applied to it. Perhaps this enables it to store information. It is thought that the recording may be replayed when the conditions are changed in some way.

Could minerals such as quartz be capable of storing information?

Without more evidence, it's difficult to view these theories as anything more than speculation.

Case study three: A VISION OF THE PAST

Date: 1901
Place: Petit Trianon, Palace of Versailles, France
Witnesses: Eleanor Jourdain and Charlotte Moberly

THE EVENTS

Charlotte Moberly

Eleanor Jourdain

Charlotte Moberly was staying with her friend Eleanor Jourdain in Paris. During a stroll around the Palace of Versailles they had a strange experience. They were walking near the Petit Trianon, the summer palace of Marie Antoinette, Queen of France at the end of the 18th century. The air was still and the trees and buildings seemed flat and lifeless, like a tapestry. Charlotte felt a sense of dreaminess weighing down upon her. Then, through the trees, she saw a man wrapped in a long, dark cloak.

As the man looked up, Charlotte shuddered. He seemed to stare right through her. The expression on his scarred face was one of evil. Charlotte and Eleanor took a path which led them away from the man.

A weighty memory

A few days later, as Charlotte was writing a letter, she felt the same sense of heaviness she had felt on the day at Versailles. She turned to Eleanor and asked, "Do you think that the Petit Trianon is haunted?"

"Yes, I do," she said. It was the first time they had spoken about it.

A sinister man wearing a cloak was standing on the steps of a round building.

The story unfolds

Three months later, the two women talked about their day at Versailles again, piecing together what they remembered about it.

Charlotte recalled passing a woman who was shaking a cloth out of a window. Then, unable to find their way to the Petit Trianon, they had asked directions from two men wearing three-cornered hats, who looked like gardeners. The men told them to go straight ahead. Further along the path, Eleanor noticed a woman and a girl standing on the steps of a cottage, though Charlotte couldn't remember seeing them.

A woman was sitting sketching on the lawn.

Running man

At the sight of the man in the dark cloak, Eleanor, like Charlotte, had felt afraid. But just then another man had appeared. His face was hot and red from running. He spoke to them in French and pointed along the path. As they started to walk in that direction, they turned to thank him, but he was no longer there.

A lady sketching

Eleanor and Charlotte crossed a bridge which brought them into view of the Petit Trianon. On the lawn, Charlotte saw a woman wearing a shady hat and a pale, old-fashioned dress. She seemed to be sketching. Eleanor, however, saw nobody. Yet as they walked across the lawn, Eleanor moved her skirts aside as if she was making room for something.

Moments later, a man ran out of a side building and showed them to the front of the palace, where a wedding party was taking place.

The Petit Trianon, a summer palace in the grounds of the Palace of Versailles

Case study three: A VISION OF THE PAST

Curiouser and curiouser

Charlotte and Eleanor were puzzled by the differences in what they had seen. They felt sure they wouldn't have missed people, as the place was so quiet. Yet Eleanor had walked right by the lady on the lawn without seeing her. Eventually, they decided to write down separate accounts, to compare their experiences.

A royal haunting

Soon afterwards, Eleanor asked a French friend whether she had heard any stories about Versailles being haunted. The friend told her that there had been reports of the ghost of Queen Marie Antoinette appearing in the garden of the Petit Trianon.

A return trip

In January 1902, Eleanor went to Versailles again. As she crossed a bridge over a stream, she felt an eerie sensation. In the distance, she saw some men filling a cart with sticks. They wore tunics and capes with pointed hoods. When she looked again, they were no longer there.

An invisible crowd

After a time, Eleanor came to some woods. She saw a figure slip into the trees. Then she heard a rustling noise beside her. Suddenly she felt closed in, as if she was surrounded by invisible people. In the distance, she could hear a band playing, but much closer she heard voices whispering.

Eleanor saw a figure slipping into the woods just ahead of her.

Dramatic changes

On later visits to Versailles, Eleanor couldn't find many of the places she had seen before. Where there had been thick woods, there were clear views. She couldn't find the building where the cloaked man had stood. Paths were laid out differently and there was no bridge. The most striking difference was that the grounds had changed from being almost deserted to being crowded with tourists and stalls.

Back in time

Charlotte and Eleanor concluded that something strange had occurred during their visits to Versailles. They began to investigate further. Their research led them to believe that what they had seen was Versailles at the time of Marie Antoinette. Their studies of maps, costumes and music of the late 18th century seemed to support this theory. Over many years, they collected enough material to publish a book about it. It was called *An Adventure*.

People from the past

Charlotte and Eleanor even found information about people of the period that seemed to correspond with those they had seen.

After looking at portraits of Marie Antoinette, Charlotte claimed that one by an artist named Wertmüller looked very much like the woman she had seen sketching.

Wertmüller's portrait of Marie Antoinette

They suggested that the man in the cloak may have been the Comte de Vandreuil, who deserted the queen shortly before her execution in 1793. He had suffered from smallpox, so his face would have been scarred like the face of the man they saw. The running man may have been a messenger sent to warn the queen that a hostile mob was approaching.

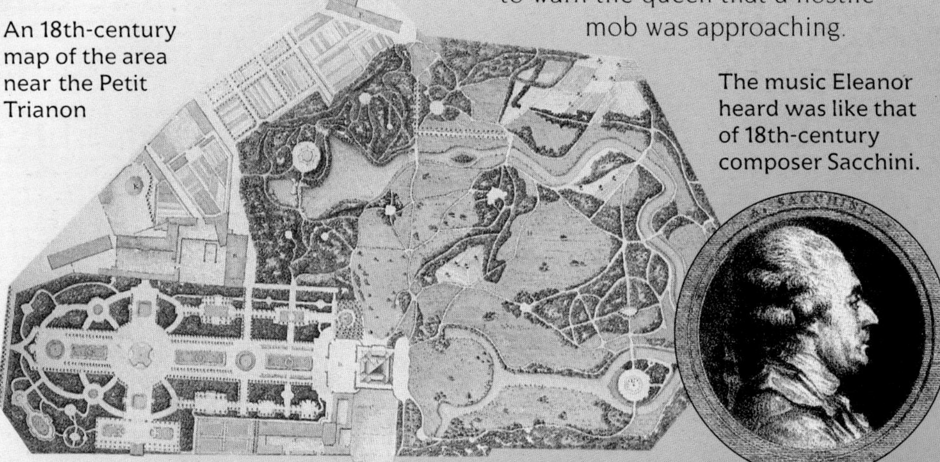

An 18th-century map of the area near the Petit Trianon

The music Eleanor heard was like that of 18th-century composer Sacchini.

Case study three: THE ASSESSMENT

Eleanor and Charlotte spent ten years gathering historical evidence to support their story. They were either very convinced by what they saw or very interested in convincing others.

Actors performing

Many people have suggested that Eleanor and Charlotte may have seen actors performing some sort of reenactment in the grounds of the palace. However, the two women claimed that they checked and that there were no such performances on that day.

More ghosts

The ghosts at Versailles were not the only ghosts that Eleanor and Charlotte claimed to have seen. In 1914, Charlotte saw a man wearing a toga in the Louvre Museum, Paris. She later identified him from paintings and other representations as the Roman emperor Constantine, and discovered that the Louvre was built on the site of a Roman road.

Were the women sensitive to the paranormal or did they just have active imaginations?

Charlotte was able to identify the emperor Constantine from images such as this mosaic.

Reputations at stake

Eleanor was principal of St. Hugh's Hall, which later became a college of Oxford University. She was well respected, and seems unlikely to have invented the story. However, she didn't choose to risk her reputation. *An Adventure* was published using the pseudonyms Frances Lamont and Elizabeth Morison.

St. Hugh's College as it is today

The story grows

When *An Adventure* was published, it was reviewed by the Society for Psychical Research (SPR), a group which studies strange phenomena. The SPR noted that the story had changed as Eleanor and Charlotte researched it. What they claimed was their first record of the events was actually a later version with extra details. For example, the "gardeners" they saw became "officials" and were later described as guards. Were the women confusing what they had seen with the results of their research?

STEPPING BACK IN TIME

There are stories, like that of the Versailles ghosts, which report not just the sighting of a ghostly figure, but an entire scene. Is the viewer experiencing an earlier time rather than a "ghost" within their own time?

A form of memory

Eleanor's and Charlotte's theory about what they saw at Versailles was that they had somehow accessed the queen's memories.

Another theory offered to explain such experiences is that the scenes are people's memories from previous lives they have lived. However, this makes the assumption that reincarnation (the soul being born into a new body after death) is possible.

A simpler explanation is that the information is from memories of events in a person's current life that they don't recall consciously.

Looking back in time

Could people find out about events from the past through looking back in time, a process known as retrocognition? Little is known about it, but some people think that the information may be obtained through ESP (extra sensory perception), a kind of sixth sense.

Time theories

People who have had these experiences may somehow have been able to travel in time. Current scientific research suggests that this may be possible. However, it is not known how it might work in practice.

Some scientists have suggested that we should think of time as a loop rather than as a line, and that it may be possible to hop across the loop to another point in time.

POLICE PUBLIC CALL BOX

BBC

In the cult British television series *Doctor Who*, this machine, known as the TARDIS, was used for time travel.

Universal (U.I.P.)

A series of films called *Back to the Future* explored the possible effects of time travel.

Case study four: THE HAUNTED HOTEL

Date: June, 1969
Place: Wales (town not recorded)
Witness: Detective Inspector D. Elvet Price

THE EVENTS

The night began with a strange incident, though at the time Inspector Price thought little of it. He had come up from London early that morning to make inquiries about a case he was working on and was spending the night at a hotel in a small Welsh town.

Just before going to bed, he had gone out to the bathroom in the corridor outside his room. On his way, he met a woman dressed in long, old-fashioned clothes. He greeted her, but she didn't respond. She continued along the corridor as if in a trance.

The inspector assumed that the woman just hadn't heard him. It was only later events that made him wonder who or what she was.

A woman walked straight past the inspector, as if in a trance.

A rude awakening

It wasn't long before Inspector Price was sleeping soundly. Some time later, he woke up suddenly, his heart pounding. Choking and gasping noises were coming from the floor beside his bed. He scrambled over to the light switch.

As he did, a strange sensation of coldness enveloped him. When he switched on the light, the noises and the sensation of coldness stopped. The room was empty.

He glanced at his watch. It was 1:30am. Feeling confused and unsettled, he slipped his wallet and watch under the pillow and settled back down to sleep.

The inspector put his wallet and watch under the pillow for safety.

A disturbing night

Despite this odd experience, the inspector slept soundly. But before long, his sleep was interrupted by the sounds of a struggle for the second time that night. Again he switched on the light and again the noises stopped. It was 3:00am.

At 4:15am he was woken up for a third time. As he listened to the blood-curdling noises, the inspector felt a clammy coldness creep over him. Then, unable to bear the horrific sound of suffering, he switched on the light. The noises ceased.

Lights on

Inspector Price had had enough. Even a long career with the police had not prepared him for such strange happenings. This time he decided to keep the light on. Eventually, exhaustion overwhelmed him and he drifted off to sleep. To his relief, when he next woke up it was morning.

Each time the inspector switched on the light, the noises stopped.

Case study four: THE HAUNTED HOTEL

Keeping quiet

The next day, Inspector Price was met by Sergeant Jones, the local policeman who had booked the hotel for him. The inspector didn't mention his strange experiences for fear he would be ridiculed. Yet he couldn't stop thinking about them.

A week later, back in London, the inspector met another policeman from the Welsh town. He was so curious about what had happened that he told him the story, but swore the man to secrecy. The man then revealed that the hotel was reported to be haunted. The story behind the haunting was a violent one.

A violent death

According to local stories, in 1909 the hotel had been the scene of an horrific and violent death. Angharad Llewellyn, the wife of the landlord, had been brutally murdered. She had been beaten and strangled in her bedroom. Inspector Price realized with a feeling of sickness and horror that the sounds he had heard must have been a bizarre replay of the woman's dying moments.

The real story

He listened in shock as the policeman told how the woman's husband had been found guilty of her murder and hanged.

In fact, when Inspector Price later researched the story himself, he discovered that the murder had taken place in 1920. He also found out that the husband had not been hanged but had received a five-year prison sentence. The judge had concluded that the man had assaulted his wife, but had not intended to kill her.

The hotel landlord killed his wife by strangling her.

Case study four: THE ASSESSMENT

The documents from the murder trial seem to offer evidence to support this sinister story. However, since the name of the town where it occurred has not been recorded, the details are difficult to confirm.

Just a dream?

During his troubled night, each time Inspector Price switched on the light, the noises stopped. Perhaps he was just having a recurrent nightmare and it was only when he switched on the light that he woke up fully. Often when we first wake up from a dream, it still seems very vivid.

Silent lady

The woman in the corridor could have been the ghost of the murder victim. A simpler explanation could be that she was just another guest or a member of the hotel staff.

Inaccurate story

Inspector Price's original interpretation of his experience as a haunting was based on local stories rather than hard facts. On closer examination, however, these stories distorted the true events to produce a more dramatic and sinister tale.

Sleepy visions

One explanation for what Inspector Price heard is that he was hallucinating. When falling asleep, people sometimes experience vivid sensations, called hypnogogic visions, which are a little like nightmares. A similar vision, known as a hypnopompic vision, can occur when waking up. These kinds of visions (or, in the inspector's case, sounds) can be very realistic and frightening. The sleeper often feels a sense of being trapped and sometimes experiences choking sensations. Perhaps the inspector mistook his own choking and gasping for that of someone else.

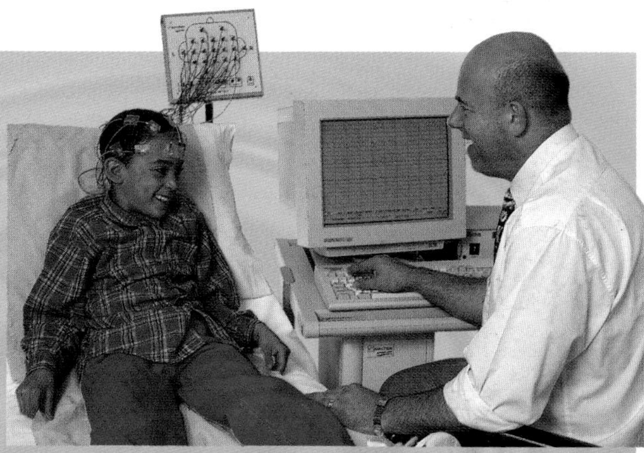

Scientists find out about people's experiences during sleep by monitoring their brain activity using an electroencephalogram (EEG) like this one.

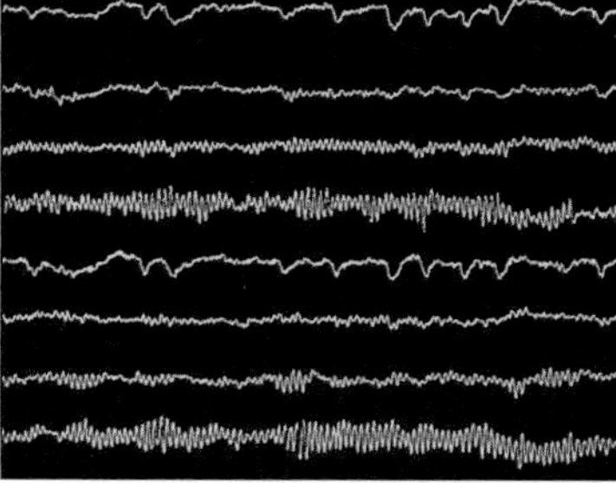

An EEG chart shows when the brain is most active.

PHOTOGRAPHING GHOSTS

Ghosts are notoriously difficult to capture on film. However, there are a few examples of photographs of "ghosts". With modern cameras and computer programs, it is easy to fake ghost photographs; but for pictures taken many years ago techniques for faking were more limited.

Transparent images

Most people who claim to have seen ghosts describe them as solid. Yet most photographs of ghosts show transparent figures like the one below, known as the Brown Lady.

The ghostly Brown Lady of Raynham Hall

The Brown Lady was photographed at Raynham Hall in 1936 by Captain Provand and Indre Shira. As the photograph was taken, Indre saw a figure, but the captain saw nothing. Perhaps Indre tampered with the photograph in order to convince him.

Great-grandmother visits

In 1991, Greg Maxwell pointed up into the air as his photograph was taken and said "Old Nana's here". When the photograph was developed, Greg's family recalled his remark and concluded that the white shape in the photograph was the ghost of his great-grandmother.

Greg and "Nana", 1991

The fuzzy shape in the photograph could be anything – a reflection from a light or a finger over the camera lens. What makes it seem significant is Greg's comment and his attentive gaze.

A fiery girl

When developed, this photograph of a fire at Wem Town Hall, Shropshire, in 1995, revealed a young girl. People suggested she was the ghost of a girl who caused a fire there in 1677, when her candle set light to the roof.

Analysts have suggested that the figure may be an optical illusion caused by shadows of the flames and falling wood. Or it might be a double exposure, which means two separate pictures have been combined on a single piece of film. Nevertheless, the final result makes a convincing ghost photograph.

A close-up of the mysterious girl at Wem Town Hall surrounded by flames

Tulip Staircase

When Reverend Hardy took a photograph of the Tulip Staircase in 1966, he couldn't see the eerie figures that appear on the picture.

At first glance, the figure at the bottom of the stairs looks like a hooded spirit. However, another explanation seems more likely. Reverend Hardy didn't use a flash. Instead he gave the picture a long exposure, keeping the camera's shutter open for several seconds. If, during this time, someone had dashed upstairs, their image could have been captured several times in a single picture.

Reverend Hardy's Tulip Staircase ghosts, National Maritime Museum, Greenwich

This picture, taken by photographer Brian Tremain, shows how a moving person would be captured on film.

Date: From August 23rd, 1971
Place: Bélmez de la Moraleda, Spain
Witnesses: The Pereira family and other witnesses

THE EVENTS

On August 23rd, 1971, Maria Pereira caught sight of a mark on her kitchen floor. She scrubbed at it, but it didn't fade. Over the next few days, the mark became more clearly defined and started to bear an uncanny resemblance to a face. Gradually, it grew clearer until there was no longer any doubt. A face was staring up from the floor.

Destroying faces

Maria and her husband, Juan, a farmer and shepherd, couldn't understand what was happening in their house. Sensing their fear, their son Miguel used a sledgehammer to destroy the part of the floor where the face was. But soon after, a second face began to form on another part of the floor.

The council intervenes

News of the mysterious faces soon spread around the quiet town of Bélmez. Eventually, the story came to the attention of the local council, which sent someone to cut out the faces. But tests conducted on the faces revealed nothing unusual.

Bélmez is a small town in southern Spain.

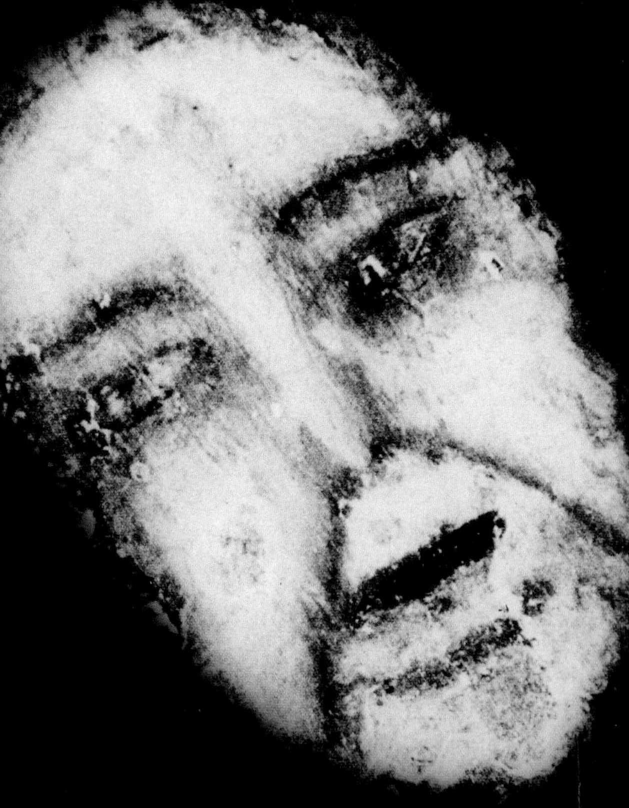

The photographs on this page show some of the faces that appeared in the floor.

The faces return

Although the mystery had not been solved, for a few days it seemed as if the Pereiras had seen the last of the faces. Then, suddenly, another one appeared. Miguel destroyed it, but as soon as the floor was repaired yet another formed. It was a woman's face, her hair flying as if caught by the wind. Around her, more faces appeared.

After a time, some of the faces faded and disappeared, but new ones appeared in their place. Sometimes small crosses appeared too.

Skeletons uncovered

The story generated a frenzy of interest. People crowded into the narrow streets of Bélmez, hoping to get a glimpse of the faces. A number of researchers became interested too. Among them was Professor de Argumosa, a lecturer at the University of Madrid. His inquiries revealed an intriguing story which might be connected with the faces. In the 17th century, a governor of the province of Granada had ordered the murders of five members of a local family.

When part of the floor of the Pereiras' house was dug up, human remains were found buried below the floor. Among them were two headless skeletons. Were these the unlucky victims of the governor, or had the remains of a local cemetery been exposed?

Monitoring changes

Professor de Argumosa conducted a simple experiment. He divided the floor into sections and took photographs of each section. He then covered the floor with foil and sealed it at the edges so that the faces could not be tampered with. When the foil was removed, he discovered that the faces had continued to change beneath it.

Changing faces

Many different faces appeared in the floor: one was a child's, another a beautiful woman's and a third a bald old man's. Their expressions would sometimes change, or other details of their appearance would alter. Parts of their bodies would occasionally appear too. One woman's hand was visible. It was holding a flower, which over a period of time became a cup.

The face known as "the bald one"

Sudden changes

Not all the changes were gradual. On one occasion, researcher José Martínez Romero, who later wrote a book about the case, saw faces appearing and disappearing at random. Others witnessed the faces forming, not over a period of days, but before their very eyes.

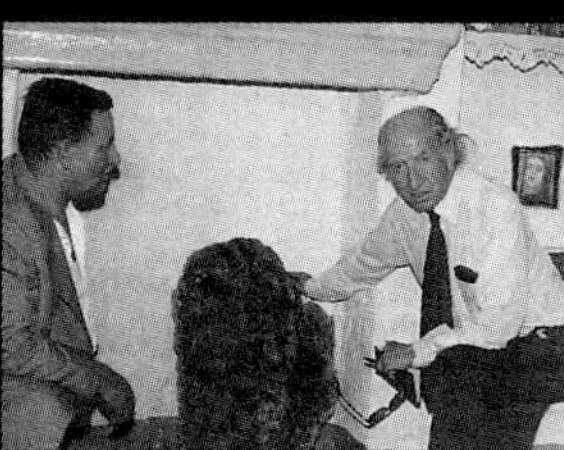

Mr. Romero and author Andrew MacKenzie examining one of the faces

Cries of the dead?

Most disturbing of all the events in the Pereiras' house were noises revealed on audio recordings made by Professor de Argumosa. No noises were heard in the room when the recordings were made, but when they were played back, terrifying cries and groans were heard mingling with murmuring voices.

Professor de Argumosa was even able to pick out a few words. He heard in Spanish what sounded like "spirits", "drunkard", "little grandchild", "Poor Cico" and "What will become of your life?". Whatever the story behind the voices, it seemed like a tragic one.

The faces of Bélmez have continued to appear for over 20 years and have been examined by numerous witnesses. Yet experts still can't agree about what they are.

Works of art

People have said that the faces look like paintings. After a chemical analysis of the faces, an inquiry led by parapsychologist J.L. Jordán concluded that this is exactly what they are. He suggested that they may have been created using soot and vinegar or cleaning chemicals. Yet there were other scientists who found no evidence of unusual chemicals.

If the faces are paintings, this does not explain how they formed before people's eyes.

Spirits of the dead

The story of the murders and the discovery of the skeletons have led to suggestions that the faces were caused by the unsettled spirits of the dead. Unfortunately, because the story dates from the 17th century, none of the faces could be identified as any of the murder victims, so it has been impossible to establish any definite connection.

Psychokinesis?

The faces seemed to be connected with Maria. She was the first to see them and they were said to be darker when she was in poor health. People wondered whether she had created the faces using her mind. This ability to influence objects mentally is known as psychokinesis. There are people who claim to have such abilities. In the 1960s, a man named Ted Serios claimed he could visualize an image, such as a building, and photograph his thought.

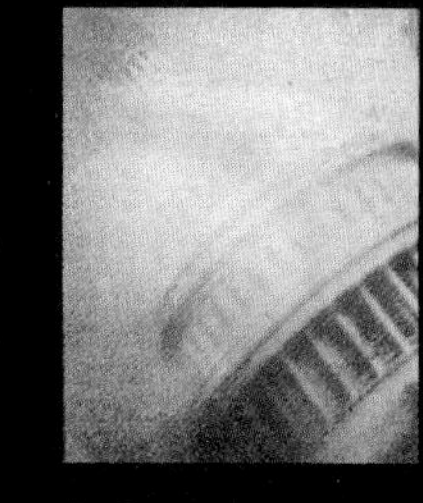

A thought photograph of the Capitol building, Washington, USA taken by Ted Serios

In the case of the Pereira family, deliberate fraud cannot be ruled out, but there is no clear evidence as to how they went about it.

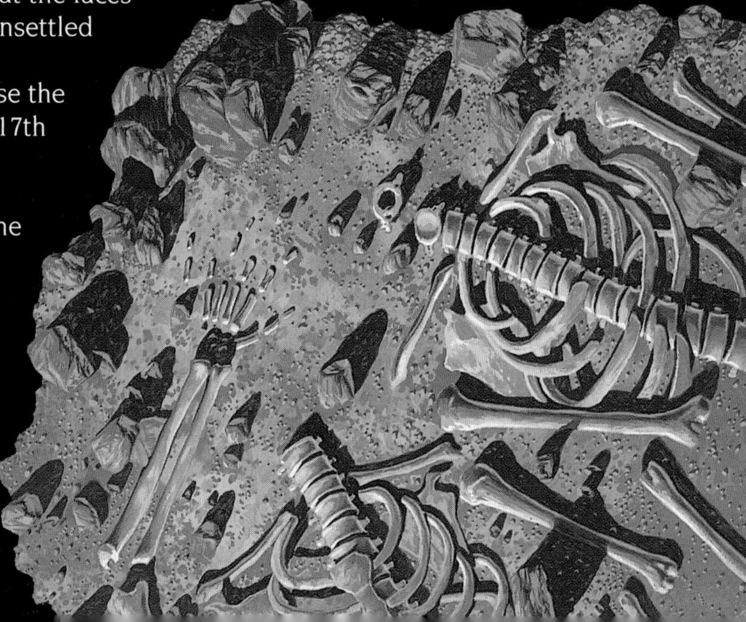

Could the skeletons under the house be connected with the mysterious faces?

Case study six: A DEADLY DISASTER

Date: 1972 – 1973
Place: Eastern Airlines' L-1011 airliners
Witnesses: Multiple witnesses

THE EVENTS

It was a moonless night in the Everglades National Park, Florida, USA. Former wildlife officer Bob Marquis was looking for frogs. As he skimmed across the expanse of reeds and water in his airboat, he noticed an airliner flying low in the sky.

Moments later, a bright orange flash cut across the night sky. Then darkness returned to the Everglades. The airliner Bob had just seen had disappeared from the sky.

Bob Marquis saw an airliner flying low above the Everglades.

The flight paths of aircraft are tracked using a radar system like this one.

At the same time, in the flight control room at Miami airport, Charles Johnson noticed that flight 401 was no longer appearing on the radar system. The full horror of the situation soon became clear to him. The plane had plummeted into a remote part of the Everglades.

Crash horror

Meanwhile, Bob Marquis guessed that the plane must have crashed and realized that he was probably the only person for miles around. With only a small lamp tied around his head to guide him, he turned his tiny airboat and set off in what he thought was the direction of the crash. But this was only the beginning of a long and eerie story.

Guiding light

The sound of hysterical screams and cries of agony guided Bob to the site of the crash. As he moved his head, the flickering beam of his lamp picked out the pale, frightened faces of the living, and the limp bodies of the dead.

Bob felt desperately alone. The icy water was shallow, but it seemed ominous as it washed over the survivors trapped in the wreckage. He tried to help people, but the tall grass and the weight of the water held him back as he waded among the jagged remains of the aircraft. It seemed an eternity before help came.

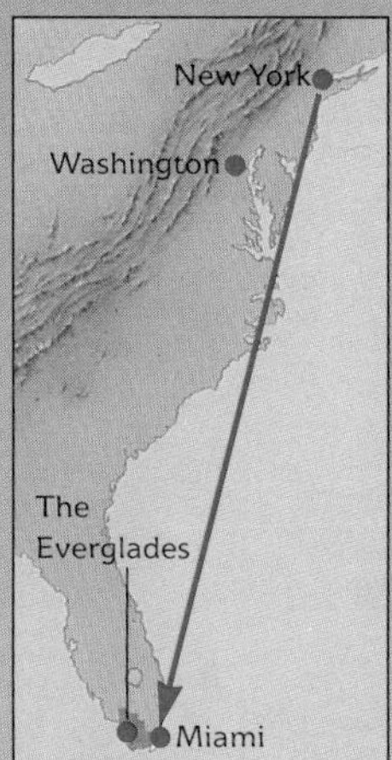

The flight path of the doomed plane

An inquiry

Of the 176 people on board flight 401 on December 29th, 1972, only 75 survived.

In the weeks after the crash, the National Transportation Safety Board began to piece together what had happened that night. At first, the cause of the crash was a mystery. The crew had been having minor technical problems, but seemed to have them under control. The flight controller's only clue that something was wrong was a radar reading just before the crash which showed that the plane was flying unusually low.

The debris from the plane had been hurled in all directions.

Rescue workers used airboats to reach the survivors of the crash.

Case study six: A DEADLY DISASTER

Who was to blame?

Gradually, a fuller picture of what had happened emerged. The inquiry into the disaster concluded that the crew had been distracted by technical problems shortly before the crash. However, other problems with the information on their displays may also have contributed to the disaster.

The most significant revelation was that a safety device that allowed the pilot to override the plane's automatic pilot system in an emergency had been badly designed. This meant that the automatic pilot could be disengaged accidentally by someone leaning across the controls.

The final moments

The co-pilot's computer and the captain's had different settings. This may have meant that the co-pilot's display did not show a change in altitude when the automatic pilot disengaged. The captain's controls did show this information, but the captain didn't notice it.

It was only in the final few seconds before the crash that the co-pilot realized that something was wrong. "We did something to the altitude," he said. Then a moment later he called out, "Hey, what's happening here?" But it was too late.

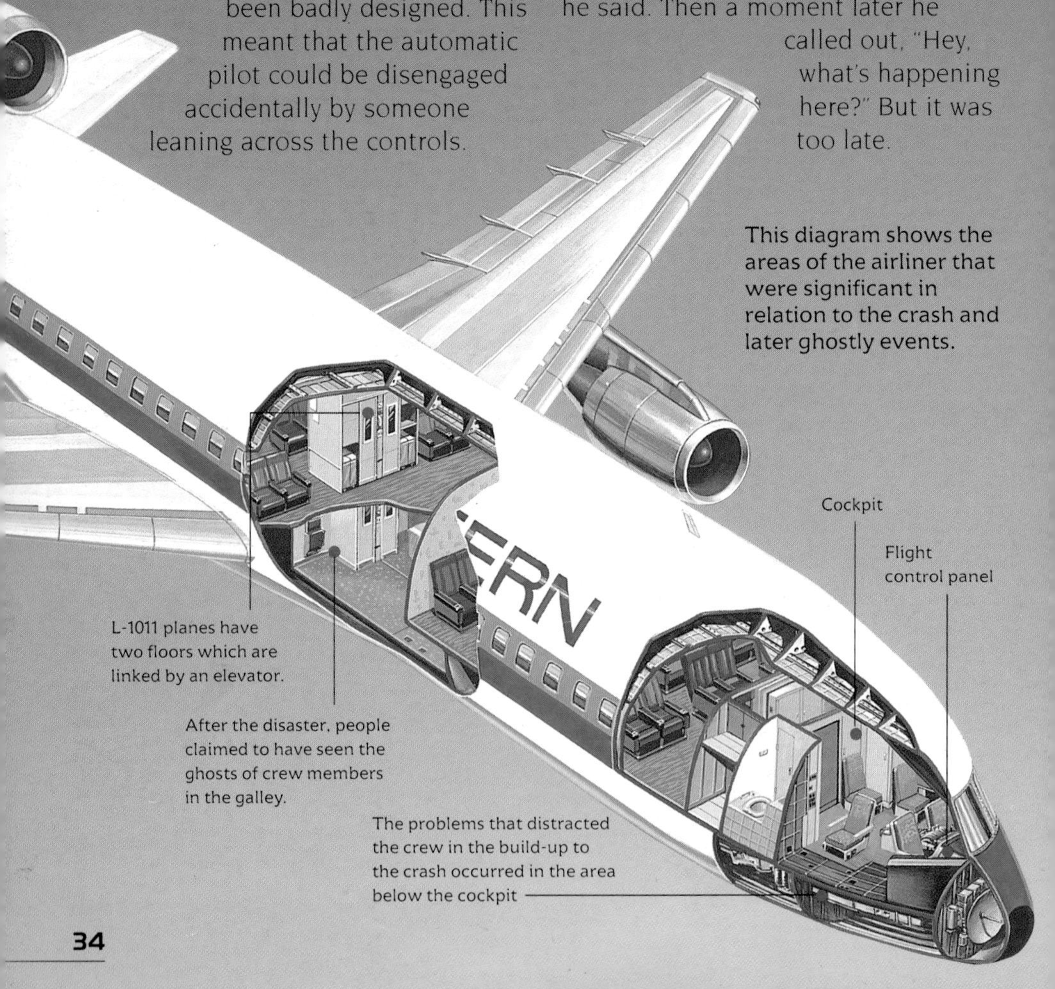

This diagram shows the areas of the airliner that were significant in relation to the crash and later ghostly events.

Cockpit

Flight control panel

L-1011 planes have two floors which are linked by an elevator.

After the disaster, people claimed to have seen the ghosts of crew members in the galley.

The problems that distracted the crew in the build-up to the crash occurred in the area below the cockpit

A disappearing passenger

In the weeks after the accident, some unusual stories began to circulate. On a number of L-1011 planes (the same kind of plane as the one that had crashed), people claimed to have seen the ghosts of the crew members who had died on flight 401. A passenger on one flight sat beside a man wearing a flight engineer's uniform. He looked pale, so she asked how he was. He didn't respond. The woman called the stewardess over. But when she came, the man disappeared.

Don Repo was the engineer on flight 401.

The passenger became hysterical and began to scream. Nothing the stewardess said could console the terrified woman. She demanded to see photographs of all Eastern Airways' flight engineers. From these, she was able to identify the man she had seen. It was Don Repo, the engineer who died on flight 401.

A strange mist

On another flight, a stewardess was in the galley waiting for the elevator when she caught sight of a hazy cloud nearby. It seemed to be pulsating. She stabbed urgently at the elevator button. She had heard some of the stories and had no desire to remain there on her own.

As she waited, she tried not to look at the shape. But, out of the corner of her eye, she saw it form into a face. She could even see a pair of steel-rimmed glasses appearing. Eventually, the elevator came and she made her escape.

Gradually the cloud formed into a face.

Captain Loft's face was staring down from an overhead locker.

Face to face

Some Eastern Airlines' staff who had known Captain Loft and Don Repo personally reported seeing their ghosts. One flight attendant opened an overhead locker to find Captain Loft's face staring at her.

On another occasion, a captain and two flight attendants spotted Captain Loft sitting in the first class section of a plane.

In a sighting on another flight, a senior Eastern Airlines' representative started to talk to someone he thought was the flight's captain. He had been speaking for some time before he realized he was talking to Bob Loft.

A ghostly protector

The ghost of engineer Don Repo seemed to want to watch over other flights. It said to one captain, "There will never be another crash of an L-1011 . . . we will not let it happen."

Another time, he told an engineer about to conduct a preflight check, "You don't need to worry about the preflight. I've already done it."

Near disaster

On another flight, crew members saw the face of Don Repo appear in an oven door. It gave a warning that was to prove uncannily close to the mark: "Watch out for fire on this plane."

On the next part of their journey, the crew had problems with two of the three engines and had to land the plane using the one remaining engine. They brought it down safely, but could this have been because Don Repo was looking after them?

A dusty old mansion seems a more typical location for a haunting than a large airliner, yet people frequently claim to have seen apparitions in such modern environments.

Anonymous witnesses

During the research for his book, *The Ghost of Flight 401*, John Fuller interviewed many people who claimed to have seen the ghostly crew members. Most witnesses were people who worked on other flights.

It is claimed that Eastern Airlines put pressure on their employees not to talk about their encounters. As a result, most witnesses preferred to remain anonymous. Unfortunately this makes it difficult to check their accounts.

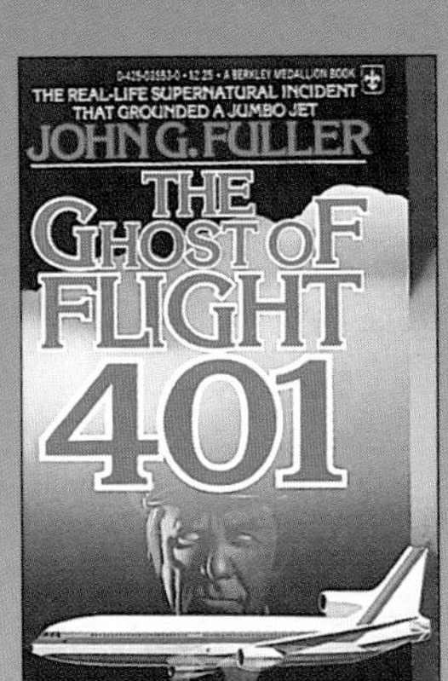

John Fuller's book, *The Ghost of Flight 401*

Expecting a ghost

The ghostly sightings all took place on L-1011 airliners, the same model as the one that crashed. Following the crash, passengers and crew members on these Eastern Airlines flights were probably anxious and preoccupied with the disaster. Crew members may also have been suffering from grief, after the deaths of their colleagues.

The combination of these factors, together with the stories about ghosts being circulated, may have prepared people's imaginations for ghostly occurrences, causing them to hallucinate or to misinterpret shadows in poor lighting as faces.

Missing log books

Some of the ghostly sightings were supposedly recorded by crew members in flight log books, where anything that happens on the flight is noted down. Unfortunately, these log books disappeared mysteriously. It is claimed that senior Eastern Airlines' staff often asked for log books to be replaced before previous log books were full. Were the witnesses' reports being hushed up, or was the story merely an excuse for the absence of this crucial evidence?

Kim Basinger and Ernest Borgnine in the movie *The Ghost of Flight 401*

Paramount TV

Case study seven: A GHOSTLY DOUBLE

Date: 1845 – 1846
Place: Neuwelcke, Latvia
Witnesses: Multiple witnesses

THE EVENTS

The girls barely showed any surprise when their teacher's double appeared at the blackboard beside her, mimicking her actions. Such events had become a common occurrence in Emelie Sagée's classes.

Seeing double

Only the previous week, the whole school had been distracted by a similar incident. One of Emelie's students was gazing out of the classroom window, when she noticed her teacher sitting outside in the garden with a group of girls. Nothing strange about that, except that Miss Sagée was also sitting inside, in that very classroom.

The girl nudged the person next to her. Gradually, a wave of whispering and shuffling spread across the classroom. Soon everyone in the class was on their feet, crowding around the window.

Reaching out

Two of the students in the classroom were bold enough to reach out and touch their teacher's double. They felt only the slightest resistance as their fingers touched it, as if brushing against fine fabric. Then, as one of them walked in front of Emelie's chair, she passed right through the apparition.

On one occasion Emelie's double appeared beside her at the blackboard.

In two places

Later, Emelie explained to the principal how she had been in the garden when she had noticed that a class indoors was unattended. She had thought that someone ought to be supervising the class. It was as if Emelie's desire to be in two places at once had somehow been fulfilled.

The girls who had been with Emelie in the garden recalled that she had looked tired. It was as if the effort involved in producing a double was weakening the "real" Emelie.

A mysterious reflection

On another occasion, a pupil named Antoinette von Wrangel fainted in fright when she looked in a mirror and caught sight of both Emelie and her double straightening their dresses.

Double trouble

Gossip about Emelie's antics soon spread. The stories were damaging the school's reputation and so eventually Emelie was asked to leave. It was only then that Emelie revealed that this was the 19th job that she had lost due to the appearances of her second self.

This painting from 1855 shows the kind of school where Emelie taught.

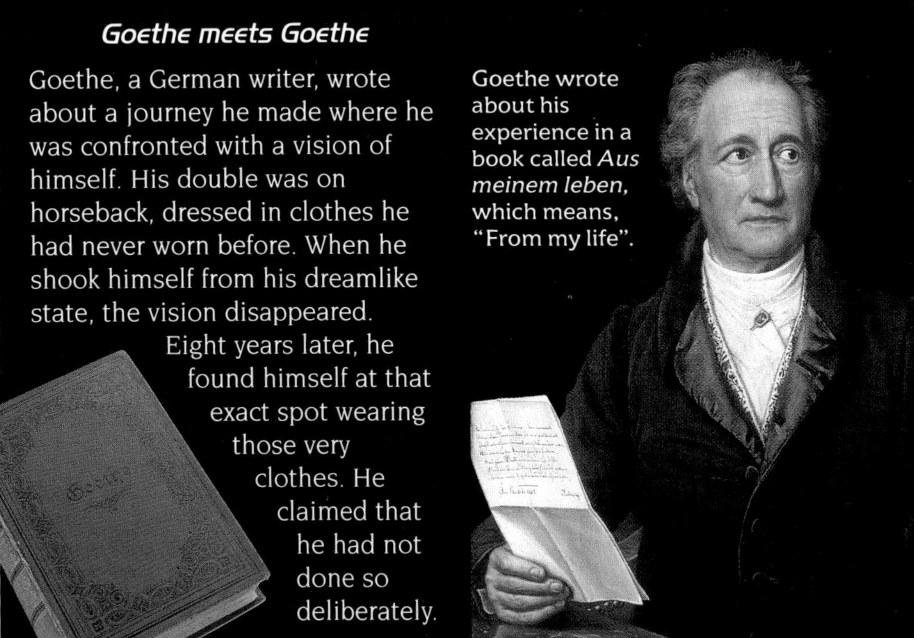

Goethe meets Goethe

Goethe, a German writer, wrote about a journey he made where he was confronted with a vision of himself. His double was on horseback, dressed in clothes he had never worn before. When he shook himself from his dreamlike state, the vision disappeared.

Eight years later, he found himself at that exact spot wearing those very clothes. He claimed that he had not done so deliberately.

Goethe wrote about his experience in a book called *Aus meinem leben,* which means, "From my life".

Case study seven: THE ASSESSMENT

If the story of Emelie Sagée's double is true, what was this "ghost" of a living person?

An out-of-body experience

It's possible that Emelie's double may be connected to something called an out-of-body experience (or OBE). Some people, who claim to have experienced an OBE, say that they felt their mind "leave" their body. One theory offered to explain what happens during an OBE is that people have a non-physical, or astral, body which is somehow separated from their physical body.

During an OBE, a person's astral body is believed to separate from their physical body.

Schoolgirl trick?

Although Emelie's double was supposedly seen by many people, the story seems to have been passed down by just one of her students, a girl named Julie von Güldenstubbe. Could she have exaggerated something that happened, or even made the whole thing up?

In the mind

Often people who see their double are simply hallucinating. Hallucination is associated with certain mental illnesses, but it is also common for people who are not ill to hallucinate. Hallucination seems an unlikely explanation in Emelie's case, because there were several witnesses. However, they may have had some sort of collective hallucination.

Wish fulfilment

In 1881, the Society for Psychical Research (see page 20) received an account from a man named Mr. Beard who claimed that by concentrating he had been able to make an image of himself appear in his fiancée's house some distance away. The image was seen by his fiancée and her sister.

Interestingly, it was when Emelie was worried about the supervision of a group of pupils that her double appeared. Could her desire to be in two places have caused her to project an image of herself?

WHEN A GHOST ISN'T A GHOST

Late one night, in the laboratory where he worked, Vic Tandy began to feel uncomfortable. It was cold, but he was sweating. Out of the corner of his eye, he saw a figure moving across the floor. As he turned to face it, it faded and disappeared. Vic was not the only person to have seen strange things in the laboratory and people had begun to suggest it might be haunted.

Mysterious vibrations

The next day, Vic brought his fencing blade into the laboratory to repair it. He placed it in a vice and went off to get some oil.

When he returned, the blade was vibrating dramatically. Feeling puzzled, he began to investigate further.

The fencing blade was vibrating without any obvious cause.

Sound energy

The blade vibrated most in the middle of the room. Vic's engineering experience led him to think that the vibrations were caused by a low frequency sound, known as infrasound, which is below the range of human hearing.

Tests revealed that vibrations from a new fan in the room had caused a sound wave which was trapped in the room. Once the fan was moved, the "ghost" was not seen again.

A scientific explanation

With this information, Vic began to put together a scientific explanation for what he had seen. His efforts show that a ghost story may have an ordinary explanation.

Vic read a report which indicated that infrasound may cause people to sweat, shiver and have breathing difficulties. This could explain his unease just before he saw the ghost.

Vic also found out that vibrations from a low frequency sound can cause the human eyeball to vibrate. If this happened to his eye in the laboratory, Vic's vision may have become blurred, causing him to see the strange shape out of the corner of his eye.

A vibrating eyeball could make people think they have seen a ghost.

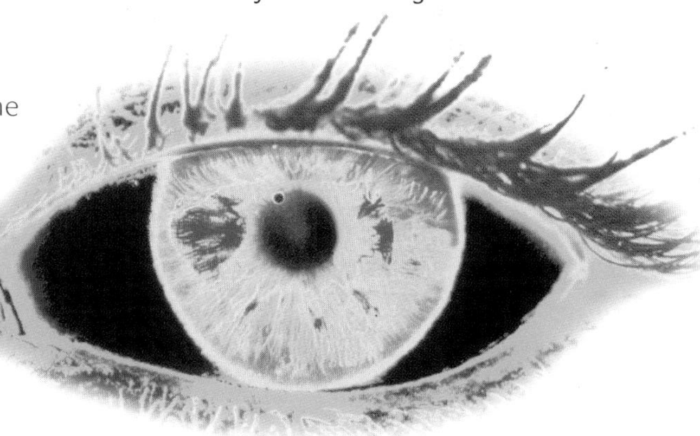

Case study eight: GHOSTS OF THE ROAD

Every year, distressed motorists report strange things that have happened to them on the road. Here is a selection of typical experiences. Is the most likely explanation for them a ghostly one?

Case: VANISHING ACT
Date: October 12th, 1979
Place: Stanbridge, England
Witness: Roy Fulton

THE EVENTS

Roy Fulton was on his way back from a darts match when he noticed a man hitchhiking at the side of the road. Roy was alone in the car, but it was a dark, foggy night, so he decided to pull over to offer the man a lift.

Roy Fulton (middle) and some friends in his local pub

Roy picked up the hitchhiker in Stanbridge.

A silent stranger

As soon as Roy stopped, the man climbed into the van without saying a word. When asked where he wanted to go, the man didn't speak; he simply pointed up the road. Roy thought the man was acting oddly, but since he obviously didn't want to talk, Roy just kept his eyes fixed on the road ahead.

After a few minutes of silence, Roy felt he had to say something. He turned to offer the stranger a cigarette. But when he looked around, there was nobody there.

Roy stopped the van and peered into the back. He stared back along the deserted road. He couldn't understand how the man could have got out of the moving vehicle without him noticing.

Speedy escape

A sense of fear spread over him. Feeling his fingers tighten on the steering wheel, he suddenly had an overwhelming desire to get away. He made straight for the police station. The police sent a car to the scene, but found nothing. Since no crime had been committed, there was nothing more they could do.

Case: A WARNING MESSAGE
Date: May 20th, 1981
Place: Palavas-les-Flots, France
Witnesses: Multiple witnesses

THE EVENTS

Four friends were driving back from the beach when they saw a woman on the road ahead. Her pale raincoat reflected the glare from the headlights, giving her a sinister air.

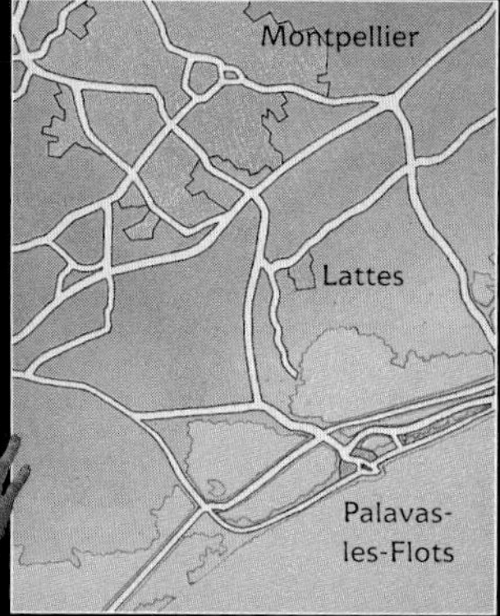

Montpellier and the surrounding area

A figure in a white raincoat was standing in the road.

Tight squeeze

The driver wound down the window and called out, "We're heading for Montpellier". The woman nodded.

The car was a Renault 5 with only two doors, so the driver got out to let the new passenger in. She clambered in without speaking, wedging herself between the two women in the back.

A disappearance

Anxious to get home, the driver started to accelerate. As the car picked up speed, the stranger shouted, "Look out for the bend. You are risking your life!".

The driver braked, just as the road swerved into a sharp bend. The women screamed. Their companion had gone.

In shock

When the car came to a halt, the four friends sat still in shock and confusion. Then, at a loss for what else to do, they went to the Montpellier police. Gradually Inspector Lopez began to feel unsettled by their story. "Their panic wasn't put on and we soon realized they were genuine."

Case: SCENE OF AN ACCIDENT
Date: July 12th, 1974, and November 8th, 1992
Place: Bluebell Hill, Kent, England
Witnesses: Maurice Goodenough and Ian Sharpe

THE EVENTS

It was just after midnight on July 12th, 1974. Maurice Goodenough was driving along the lonely Bluebell Hill road. Suddenly a figure appeared in front of his car. He braked, but it was too late. The car smashed straight into it. When he ran to the front of the car, he found a young girl lying motionless on the road, her forehead bleeding. She only looked about ten years old.

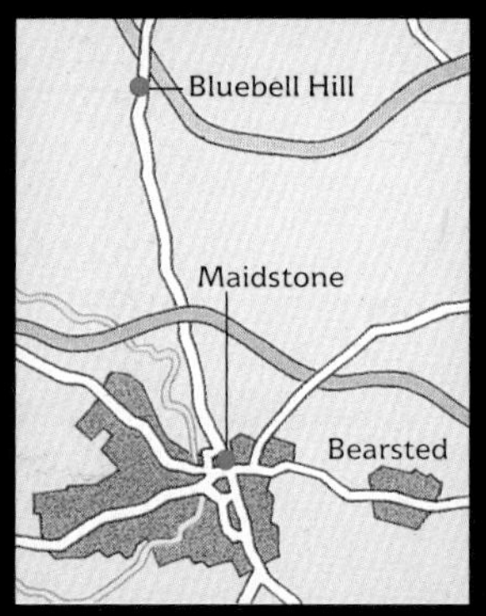

This map shows the location of Bluebell Hill.

A terrible accident

Maurice was trembling as he carried the girl to the side of the road. He found a blanket in his car and used it to cover her. There were no phones nearby.

Maurice tried to stop several cars, but nobody would stop. He didn't want to move the girl again, but she needed urgent help. He decided to drive to the police station.

The police drove to the scene of the accident immediately. They found the blanket lying at the edge of the road, but there was no sign of the girl.

No sign of life

The police searched for a body, but found nothing. When they examined the blanket, they found no bloodstains. There were no subsequent reports of a missing child in that area. Who, or what, Maurice injured remains an unsolved mystery.

All that the police found was a crumpled blanket lying at the side of the road.

Double take

18 years later, in November 1992, another driver experienced a similar horror on Bluebell Hill.

Ian Sharpe was driving along when suddenly a girl appeared. She was running toward his car. She stared straight at him and then fell underneath the car. It all happened so quickly that Ian barely had time to brake.

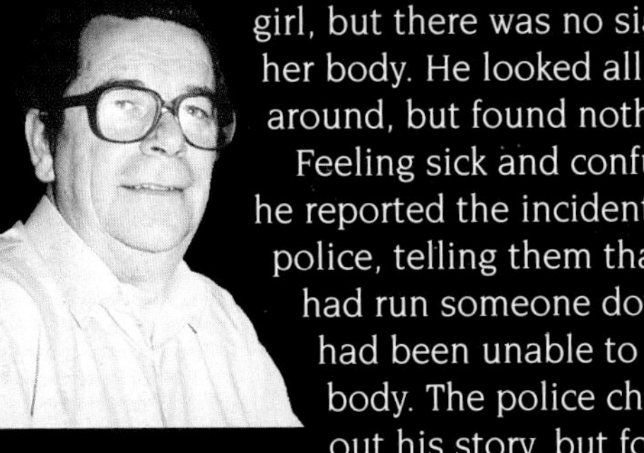

Ian Sharpe

Missing person

Numb with fear and dread, he got out of the car and kneeled down in front of it. He was certain he had killed the girl, but there was no sign of her body. He looked all around, but found nothing.

Feeling sick and confused, he reported the incident to the police, telling them that he had run someone down but had been unable to find a body. The police checked out his story, but found no sign of an accident.

Knowing the reputation of the area, the police suggested that Ian might have seen a ghost. He was doubtful: "I know I wasn't seeing things. I definitely saw a girl, and she looked human, not like a ghost with pale skin."

The girl stared straight at the car just before it hit her.

Case study eight: THE ASSESSMENT

The distinction between fact and fiction in accounts of ghosts of the road is often blurred. The unknown origin of hitchhikers makes them an appropriate subject for ghost stories.

Accidental links

Ghost stories are often linked to accidents. For example, the Bluebell Hill stories have been linked with an accident in 1965. 22-year-old Susan Browne and two friends were killed in a car crash on the night before her wedding. However, the facts don't fit the story very well: Maurice Goodenough describes a girl of about ten years old.

Judith Lingham, a friend of the bride-to-be, who died shortly after the crash

The accident at Bluebell Hill

Hallucination

The spooky atmosphere on lonely roads could lead people to imagine ghosts. Alternatively, they may be hallucinating. A tired motorist driving late at night might start to drift into sleep. In the state between waking and sleeping, people sometimes have hypnogogic visions (see page 25).

Urban myths

These stories may be "urban myths" – stories which are told again and again but which have never been proven. Usually the story is about "a friend of a friend", but often the exact source is difficult to trace.

There are recurrent themes in such stories, such as the ghost leaving an article of clothing or giving an address. Often such details seem to make the stories more believable. Yet a story like Roy Fulton's seems more convincing because it is unresolved.

A scene from the film *The Hitcher* where the figure of the hitchhiker is very sinister

INVESTIGATING A HAUNTING

The term "haunting" describes ghosts that appear more than once in a particular place. A haunting provides researchers with the opportunity to investigate a ghost for themselves.

Sensitives and sceptics

One method of investigation that researchers use is to send two groups of people into an apparently haunted location: a group of "sensitives" – people who claim to be able to detect paranormal influences, and a group of "sceptics" – people who don't believe in ghosts.

Each person is given a detailed plan of the building. They are asked to go around the house, marking on the plan the areas they feel might be haunted or, in the case of sceptics, areas that they think others might say are haunted. Researchers often find a connection between the sites the testers mark and the places where the haunting is reported to have occurred.

Equipment

Researchers also use equipment to investigate hauntings. A device called an RNG (Random Number Generator) is often used. An RNG produces numbers randomly. The idea is that something paranormal might disturb its output, so that the numbers are no longer random. In addition, video cameras and tape recorders are left running to record anything unusual, and heat sensors are used to record changes in temperature.

Interpreting results

Results for areas that are reported to be haunted are often different from results for areas that are not. This might be seen to support the theory that these areas *are* haunted. In fact, all it shows is that there is something about these locations that makes people think of them as spooky.

Borley Rectory, once described as the most haunted house in Britain

INDEX

Every effort has been made to trace the copyright holders of the material in this book. If any rights have been omitted, the publishers offer to rectify this in any subsequent editions following notification. The publishers are grateful to the following organizations and individuals for their permission to reproduce material: (t=top, b=bottom, r=right, l=left)

Cover, p1 and icons Derek Stafford/Fortean Picture Library; p2 (both) Mary Evans Picture Library; p3 Mary Evans Picture Library; p4 (tr) Andreas Trottman/Fortean Picture Library; p5 (bl) ©The British Museum (br) Andreas Trottman/Fortean Picture Library; p6 ©Patrick Ottaway; p9 (tl) Adam Hart-Davis/Fortean Picture Library (b) Universal (U.I.P)/The Ronald Grant Archive; p10 Photograph by Mark Gunn; p11 Photograph by Mark Gunn; p12 (bl) Detail by permission of the British Library 1007628.011 - the image has been digitally manipulated (br) The Ancient Art and Architecture Collection Ltd; p13 (tl) Detail by courtesy of the National Portrait Gallery (tr) Janet & Colin Bord/Fortean Picture Library (br) Cromwell after the Battle of Marston Moor (oil on canvas) by Ernest Crofts (1847-1911) Towneley Hall Art Gallery and Museum, Burnley, Lancashire/Bridgeman Art Gallery, London/New York; p14 (tr) By permission of the British Library 1007628.011 (b) Clive Barda/Performing Arts Library; p15 (bl) Universal (U.I.P)/The Ronald Grant Archive; p16 (tr) Mary Evans/Society for Psychical Research (br) Mary Evans/Society for Psychical Research; p17 ©Photo RMN/Arnaudet; p18 (bl) Tony Stone Images/Michael Busselle; (tr)Statens Konstmuseeer, Sweden (bl) ©Photo RMN (br) Lebrecht Collection; p20 (tr) Patricia Carter (b) St. Sophia/Werner Forman Archive; (t) Permission from BBC Photograph Library (br) Universal (U.I.P)/The Ronald Grant Archive; p22 Wallcovering reproduced by kind permission of Crown Wallcoverings, a division of The Imperial Home Decor Group (UK) Limited, Darwen, England; p25 (both) Science Photo Library; p26 (bl) Fortean Picture Library (br) Marina Jackson/Fortean Picture Library; p.27 (tr) Tony O'Rahilly/Fortean Picture Library (bl) Mary Evans/Peter Underwood (br) National Maritime Museum, Greenwich, London; p28 Dr Elmar R. Gruber/Fortean Picture Library; p29 (both) Dr Elmar R. Gruber/Fortean Picture Library; p30 (bl) With permission from Andrew MacKenzie (tr) With permission from José Martínez Romero; p31 Mary Evans/John Cutten; p.32 (bl) Lockheed Martin/TRH Pictures (b) UPI/Corbis (tr) TRH Pictures; p33 (bl) UPI/Corbis (br) Popperfoto; p35 UPI/Corbis; p36 UPI/Corbis; p37 (t) Fortean Picture Library (bl) Paramount TV/The Ronald Grant Archive; p39 (tr) Interior of the Women's Department of the St. Petersburg Drawing School, 1855, (oil on canvas) by Ekaterina Nikolaevna Khilova (1827-p.1876) State Russian Museum, St. Petersburg, Russia/Bridgeman Art Library, London/New York (br) Neue Pinakothek in Munich/photo AKG London; p41 (tl) Karina A. Hoskyns © (br) Mehau Kulyk/Science Photo Library; p42 Adam Hart-Davis/Fortean Picture Library; p45 (t) Frank Spooner Pictures (b) Andreas Trottman/Fortean Picture Library; p46 (tl) Frank SpoonerPictures (bl) Frank Spooner Pictures (b) Thorn EMI/The Ronald Grant Archive; p47 Fortean Picture Library

With thanks to John Russell, Chris Te-Whata, Katherine Starke, Ian McNee, Laura Creyke, Jonathan Miller, Stephen Wright, Jan McCafferty, Mark Wallace, Zöe Wray.
Thanks also to Andrew MacKenzie for information relating to case studies four and five.

First published in 1999 by Usborne Publishing Ltd, 83-85 Saffron Hill, London EC1N 8RT, England. www.usborne.com

First published in America in 1999. Printed in Spain.